# *Fun in the Sun*

**Guyla Nelson**

**and**

**Saundra Scovell Lamgo**

*Illustrated by David Grassnick
and Jonathan Chong*

*American Language Series*™
A Simple Short-Vowel Reader

MILE-HI
PUBLISHERS™

Distributed under license by
Lighthouse Publishers, LLC
PO Box 570
Greer, SC 29652
www.lighthousepublishers.com



ISBN-13  978-1-934470-05-3
ISBN-10  1-934470-05-8



Printed in China

For all boys and girls
who wish to
become readers of
good books —
and especially the
Book of Books, the Bible

# Stories

# *The Cat*

The cat is fat.

The fat cat sat.

The fat cat ran.

## *On the Red Rug*

The pup sat on the rug.

The rug is red.

The pup will nap on the red rug.

# A Rag Doll

The doll is a rag doll.

The doll has on a bib.

The doll has on a hat.

The hat is red.

# Pig in the Mud

The pig is fat.

The pig sits in the mud.

The pig has fun in the mud.

The pig is a mess.

Will the pig nap in the mud?

# *Ben*

Ben sat on a log.

Ben fell off the log.

The log is not big,

but Ben is big.

# Sam, the Cat

Sam is a fat cat.

He is tan.

Sam will get the rat.

The rat hid.

Did Sam get him?

Fat Sam got the rat.

Fat Sam will nap on the mat.

# The Cot

Nat will set up the cot.

He will set a big box on the cot.

Nat will toss a tin cup on the cot.

His red hat will be on the cot.

The cot is a mess.

Can Nat nap on the cot?

# The Van

The van is big.

Men sit in the van.

Ten men will fill the van.

The man in a tan hat runs.

He yells! He runs!

Will he miss

the van?

He runs! He yells!

Can he fit

in the van?

Did ten men

fill the van?

# Hop, Hop!

Jud will hop.
Jill will hop.
Peg will hop.

Will Nan hop?

No, No!

Nan will not hop.

# Mom's Wig

Mom has a red wig.

The red wig is in the box.

Jan will get the box.

Jan has put on Mom's red wig.

Did the red wig fit Jan?

# A Tan Bag

Pat has a tan bag.

Pat's bag is not big.

A doll will not fit in the bag.

Will a cat fit in the bag?

No, no.  A cat will not fit.

Did Pat put a mug in the bag?

No.  A mug is not in the bag.

Pat has figs in the bag.

Get a fig, Pat.

Yum, yum, yum.

# Wags, the Pup

Wags is a pup.

Wags is a tan pup.

Wags is a fat pup.

Wags has a hat.

The hat is big.

The hat will not fit Wags.

# Jim

Jim fell.

He fell in the mud.

Mud is on his red cap.

Jim has a rip in his cuff.

Mud is on his legs.

Will Mom fuss at Jim?

# *Kim*

Kim is ill.

Kim will not run.

Kim will not jog.

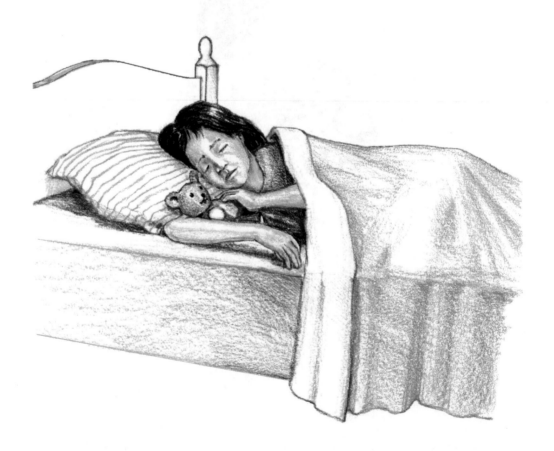

Kim will not yell.

Kim will not hum.

Kim will not get up.

Kim will nap in bed.

Kim will get well.

# Les Has His Hat

Ron has a tan cap.

Zeb has a red cap.

Les has a big hat.

The lads sat on the log.

Ron's cap fell off.

Zeb's cap fell off.

Les has his hat.

# Red Hen

Red Hen is fat.

Red Hen sits on six eggs.

Sit, Red Hen.  Sit.

Sit in the box.

Meg has a pan.

Meg will set the pan in the box by the hen.

Was Red Hen fed?

Yes, Meg fed Red Hen.

# Mud

Dad got mud
on his legs.

He got mud on his legs as
he ran in the pig pen.
The pig is a mess.
Dad is a mess.

# Pugs

Pugs tugs at the rug.

No, no, Pugs! Do not tug!

Did Pugs rip the rug?

Yes, Pugs did rip the rug.
Mom will fuss at Pugs.

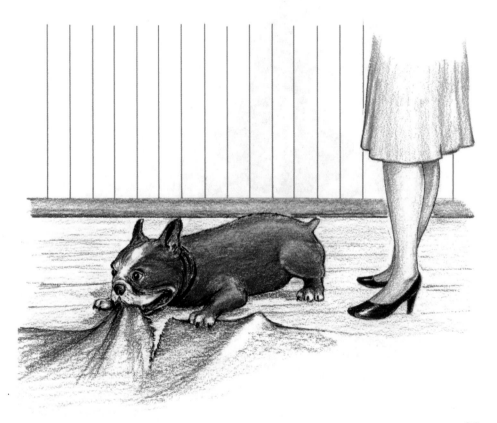

# Run, Deb, Run!

Run, Deb, run!

Run in the sun.

Run up the hill.
Run to the top.
Sit in the sun.
The sun will
be hot.
Sit, Deb, sit!

# The Ox

The ox is big.

The ox will not run.

Don sits on the big ox.

Lon sits on the big ox.

Will it be fun if the ox will not run?

# A Nap

Ned is on the bed.

Ron is on the bed.

The cat is on the bed.

The lads will nap.

Will the cat nap?

Yes.  The cat will nap on the bed.

# The Hot Sun

Max sits in the sun.

The pup is on his lap.

Max is hot.

His pup is hot.

Max gets up.

His pup gets up.

Do not run in the sun!

The sun is hot, hot, hot.

# Hum and Hop

Tom can hum.

Bob can hum.

Ted can hum.

Bev can hum.

Dan can hop.

Dan can hum.

Dan will hop as

he hums.

# A Hug and a Kiss

Ann had fun in the sun,
but Ann fell.
A leg was cut.

Mom can fix the cut leg.

Ann's leg will get well.

Ann will hug Mom.
Ann will kiss Mom.
Mom will hug Ann.

# The Tin Can

Wes will win if he hits the tin can.

The tin can is not big.

Wes hits the tin can!

Was it fun to hit the tin can?

Yes, it was fun to win.

# The Hot Pan

Mom has a pan.

The pan is hot.

Mom will set the pan on the hot pad.

Nell will not let the tot get to the hot pan.

# *Do Not Hit!*

Tim hit Sam.

He hit his pal.

It is a sin to hit a pal.

God is sad.
Mom is sad.
Dad is sad.
Tim is sad.

# The Lads

Rex has pep.

He will pass the box to Jeff.

Jeff will toss the box to Bill.

Bill will set the box by the sill.

# The Tot

The tot runs to Mom.

The tot is Mom's kin.

The tot gets a kiss.

The tot hugs Mom.

The tot is Todd.

# The Can

The lid is on the can.

The lid fits the can.

Can Mag get the lid off the can?

The lid is not off yet!

Mag will lug the can to Dad.
Dad will get the lid off.

# Gum

Dot has gum.

Rob has gum.

Sis did not get gum.

Sis is sad.

Sis is Dot's pal.

Dot ran to Sis.

Sis is not sad.

Did Sis get gum?

Yes, Sis got gum.

# The Hog Gets a Nub

Jed fed the nub to the hog.

The hog bit Jed.

Jed will sob, but the hog was fed.
The hog got a nub.

# The Cub

The cub fell off the log.
The cub ran to his den.
The den is not in the sun.

The cub's mom is in the den.

His mom will rub him.

The cub will nap in his den.

# Hats Off!

Dad will doff his hat to Mom.
Dad will doff his hat to Pam.

Dad tells Ross to doff his hat.

So Ross doffs his hat to Mom.

He doffs his hat to Pam.

# Run! Run!

Bess ran.

Sid ran.

The dog ran.

Was it fun to run?

# The Pup in the Tub

Rub-a-dub dub.

The pup is in the tub.

Rub-a-dub dub.

The tub has lots of suds.

Rub-a-dub dub.

# Kim's Tam

Kim has a gem.

The gem is on Kim's tam.

The gem sits on the top of the tam.

The gem is not dull.

# A Dab of Jam

Nan had a dab of jam.

Yum, yum.

The jam fell in Nan's lap.

Get it off, Nan!

Put a dab of jam on the bun!

# In the Bag

Mom will fix a box of nuts.

Mom will fix a cup of figs.

Mom will set the box of nuts in the bag.

Mom will set the cup of figs in the bag.

# *Sin*

Sin is bad.

God tells us not to sin.

God is sad if we sin.

If we sin, we can tell God.
God will get rid of the sin.

# A Big Badge

Madge has a badge.

The badge is big.

Dad will pin the badge on Madge.

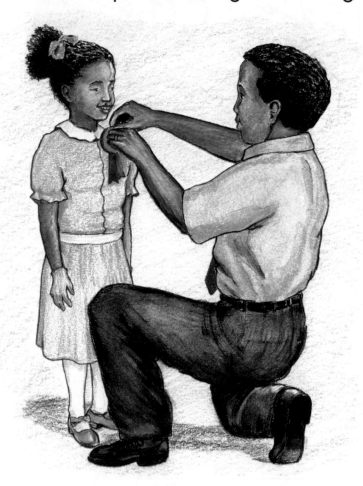

Madge will hug Dad.

Madge will kiss Dad.

# The Lodge

We will go to the lodge.
The lodge is big.
The lodge sits on the
edge of the ridge.

# The Pup on the Ledge

The pup sat on the ledge.

He sat in the hot sun.

Did the pup run?

No, the pup sat in the sun.

He did not budge.

# *The Judge*

Dad will be the judge.

He has on a big hat.

He has on a badge.

Dad has a gun.

The gun pops. We will run.

Dad will be the judge.

Will a big lad win?

# The Wedge of Fudge

Bill got a tan bag off the ledge.
The bag has a wedge of fudge in it.
The fudge has nuts in it.

## *It Bit Him!*

A bug lit on Sam's leg.

It was a big bug, and it bit him!

My, but Sam did yell!

Dad put a wet rag on Sam's leg.

He did not kill the bug.

The bug ran off.

Dad did not get the bug, but Sam's leg will get well.

# A Log Jam

Ross runs a big log mill.  He is the boss.
Ross has a son and ten men to cut tons
of logs to sell.

It is a big job to get the logs off the hill
and to the mill.

It is no fun if the logs jam.

The men will pull and tug and tip the logs to get rid of the jam.

## *A Big Hit*

Ken has a bat.

Gus has a mitt.

Rex is at the lot.

Ken is at bat.

Rex will toss to Ken.

Ken will get a big hit.

Run, Ken, run! Run in the sun!

Ken, Gus, and Rex had fun at

the lot in the sun.

## *Puff*

A pet can be lots of fun.

Dad got my pet cat at a hut by the bog.

We dub my cat Puff.

Puff begs me to fill his cup.

He sits by me.

He hops in my lap.

He rubs my legs.

He runs and has fun in the sun.
Puff is lots of fun.

# *Pat the Mud!*

Bess and Peg sit in the sun.

It is fun to put wet mud in tin lids and pat the mud.

Peg sets the lids on a ledge in the sun.

As the sun hits it, the mud will get hot.

It will not get wet.

Bess will tip a lid and tap it on top till the mud lets go of the lid.

Bess will pass the mud to Peg.

Peg will put bits of dill on top.

Was it fun to pat the mud?

# *Pals*

Rags is Ron's pet.  The big dog is Ron's pal.

Rags naps on the rug by Ron's bed.

He runs as Ron jogs.

He lets Ron pet and rub him.

He has lots of fun in the sun.

If Ron tells Rags, "Sit!" the dog sits.

If Ron will toss a bag and tell Rags, "Go, get it," Rags will not lag. He will get the bag and put it by Ron's legs.

Ron will pat Rags and hug him. Rags will wag.

It is fun to be pals.

# *Off We Go!*

"Get up!" Dad tells Dan.

"The sun is up.  We will go at six."

Dan gets up.  He will not sit on the edge of his bed.

As Dan puts on his duds, Dad sets a rod and box in the van.

Dan runs to Dad. "Will my rod and box fit?"

Dad nods. "Toss in the togs to put on if we get wet."

"The full jug has to go in, and the six cups," Mom tells Dan. "And add the ribs and buns."

Tip runs up and hops in the van.

Tip will sit in Dan's lap.

Off Dan, Tip, and Dad will go.

"Will we get bass? Will it be cod?"

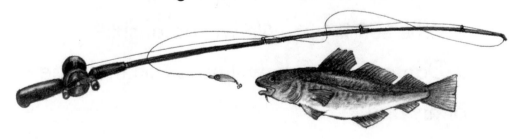

# Val

As Val naps, Mom puts a red box by the bed.

Val gets up and sits on the edge of the bed.

"To me!" yells Val.

Val pats and rubs the box.

"Is a pet in my box?" Val mulls.

"No, a pet will not fit!  A pet is so big!"

"Do not tell me!  Fudge is in the box!
Yum, yum, yum!"

"I will be Mom's Val—I will hug Mom."